IN THE NIGHT KITCHEN

MAURICE SENDAK

SCHOLASTIC INC.

New York Toronto London Auckland Sydney
Mexico City New Delhi Hong Kong

ISBN 0-439-04302-6

12 11 10 9 8 7 6 5 4 3 2   0 1 2 3/0

Printed in the U.S.A.   40

FOR SADIE AND PHILIP

DID YOU EVER HEAR OF MICKEY, HOW HE HEARD A RACKET IN THE NIGHT

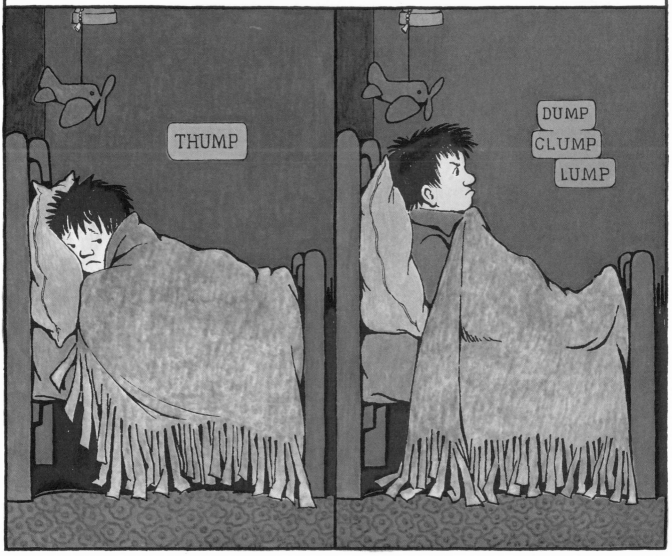

AND THEY PUT THAT BATTER UP TO BAKE

A DELICIOUS MICKEY-CAKE.

BUT RIGHT IN THE MIDDLE
OF THE STEAMING
AND THE MAKING
AND THE SMELLING
AND THE BAKING
MICKEY POKED THROUGH
AND SAID:

HE KNEADED AND PUNCHED IT
AND POUNDED AND PULLED

AND OVER THE TOP
OF THE MILKY WAY
IN THE NIGHT KITCHEN.

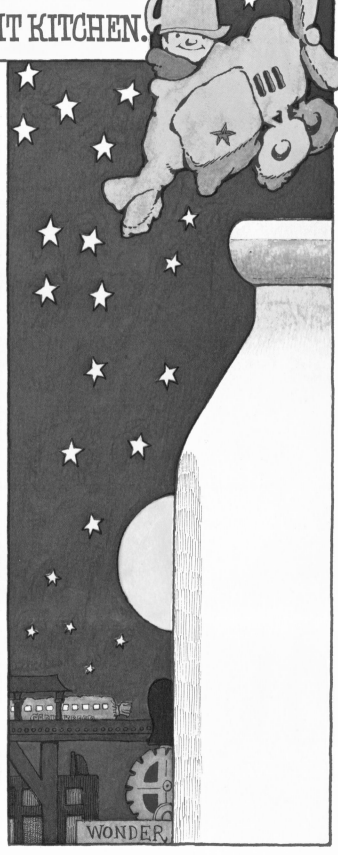

SO THE BAKERS THEY MIXED IT
AND BEAT IT AND BAKED IT.

AND THAT'S WHY, THANKS TO MICKEY WE HAVE CAKE EVERY MORNING